BRIAN the DANCING LION

by Tom Tinn-Disbury

CAPSTONE EDITIONS
a capstone imprint

For Mum, inside you're dancing. —TTD

Published by Capstone Editions,
an imprint of Capstone.
1710 Roe Crest Drive
North Mankato, Minnesota 56003
capstonepub.com

Library of Congress Cataloging-in-Publication Data
Names: Tinn-Disbury, Tom, author, illustrator.
Title: Brian the dancing lion / Tom Tinn-Disbury.
Description: North Mankato, Minnesota : Capstone Editions, an imprint of Capstone, [2022] | Audience: Ages 4-8. | Audience: Grades K-1. | Summary: Brian the lion loves to dance, but since lions are supposed to be fierce he hides his talent from his lion friends—until they explain that they also have talents that are not particularly fierce.
Identifiers: LCCN 2021020994 (print) | LCCN 2021020995 (ebook) | ISBN 9781684464241 (hardcover) | ISBN 9781684464395 (pdf) | ISBN 9781684464418 (kindle edition) Subjects: LCSH: Lion-Juvenile Fiction. | Dance-Juvenile Fiction. | Stereotypes (Social psychology)-Juvenile Fiction. | Individuality-Juvenile Fiction. | Picture books for children. | CYAC: Lion-Fiction. | Jungle animals-Fiction. | Dance-Fiction. | Stereotypes (Social psychology)-Fiction. | Individuality-Fiction. | LCGFT: Picture books. Classification: LCC PZ71.T573 Br 2022 (print) | LCC PZ71.T573 (ebook) | DDC [E]-dc23
LC record available at https://lccn.loc.gov/2021020994
LC ebook record available at https://lccn.loc.gov/2021020995

Designed by Nathan Gassman

Printed and bound in China 4545

Brian **loved** to dance.

No matter the beat or the rhythm, music made him move.

Dynamic disco music.

Calming classical music.

Funky soul music.

Dancing made Brian feel great, but he never told anyone.
Lions were meant to be brave and strong and fierce.
Nobody would think a dancing lion was brave or strong or fierce.

When his friends would ask him,
"What will you be doing tonight, Brian?
Something strong and brave and fierce, no doubt."

Brian always replied the way they expected.

One morning, Brian was walking through the jungle when he came across a couple of gazelles dancing a cha-cha.

"What's all this?" he asked the gazelles.

"We're practicing for the big dance competition," they replied. "Probably not a big, brave lion's cup of tea."

"Obviously," Brian hastily replied.
"What nonsense! Good day to you both!"

But he whispered to himself, "**This could be my chance!** If I can win, then maybe everyone will see that it's okay for lions to dance. Dancing lions are still brave and strong and fierce."

Brian practiced day . . .

and night.

It was tricky having to keep such a big secret from his friends,
but Brian imagined what would happen if they found out.

As the big competition approached, Brian was discussing techniques for being brave and strong and fierce with his friends. He could see other animals practicing their dance routines, and he could hear the inspiring music.

Brian's foot started tapping.
Before he knew it, the beat had taken over.

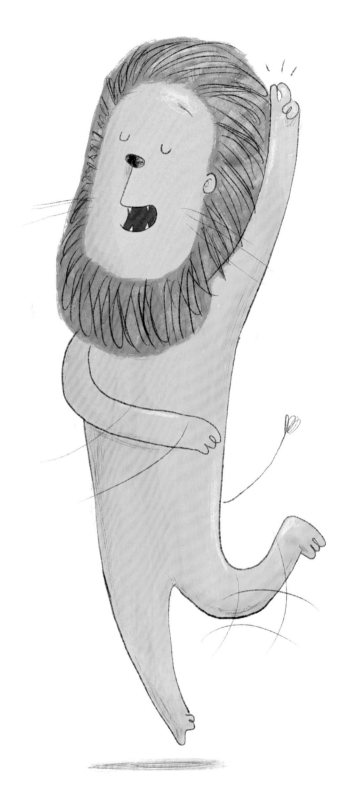

Brian had gone into full-on **dance mode!**

Brian stopped.

He gave a small roar of embarrassment and ran
as fast as he could back to his den.

A few days passed, but Brian felt too miserable
and too embarrassed to see his friends.

He hid out in his den.

Then, one day, he heard his friends outside calling to him.
Reluctantly, Brian opened the door.

Jim **loved** to stitch and sew,
designing fantastic clothes and costumes.

Betty **loved** crafting,
painting, and building things.

And Barry **loved** to sing opera.

Brian was so relieved. He also felt a bit silly.
Surely he knew deep down that his friends would be happy for him.

That's what friends are for!

"I still missed the dance competition though," he sighed.

His friends all looked at each other and smiled.
"Yes, but we have an idea . . ."

The next evening, the four friends were proud to unveil their dance spectacular. And Brian danced.

His dance was **brave**
and **strong**
and **fierce**
and **beautiful.**

Just like him.